Published by Advance Publishers, L.C.
Maitland, FL 32751 USA
www.advancepublishers.com
Produced by Judy O Productions, Inc.
Designed by SunDried Penguin

Printed in the United States of America

First published 2003.

Nemo was a little clownfish with one weak fin, which his father, Marlin, fondly called his "lucky fin." Marlin was overprotective of his son and worried about him starting school. In fact, on Nemo's first day of school, when the class headed off on a trip to the Drop-off, Marlin followed to make sure nothing happened to Nemo.

At the Drop-off, Nemo sneaked away with his new friends. When they dared Nemo to swim out to a boat anchored overhead, Nemo hesitated. Then Marlin arrived and scolded him. Nemo, embarrassed in front of his friends, defiantly swam to the boat when his dad wasn't looking. Suddenly, he was caught in a net by a diver and taken away in the boat!

Marlin raced after the boat, but it was too fast. He swam into a busy fish stream and asked if anyone had seen a boat, but no one would stop to help him. Finally, he bumped into a friendly fish named Dory, who had a short-term memory problem. She said she'd help him find his son, but forgot who Marlin was right away! Then, just as Marlin was leaving to keep searching for Nemo, he came face to face with Bruce, a very large great white shark!

Bruce took Marlin and Dory to a fish-eaters anonymous meeting. At the shark's submarine headquarters, Marlin found a diver's mask – it belonged to the diver who'd taken Nemo! Unfortunately, Marlin could not read the address written on the mask. Then Bruce got hungry and Marlin and Dory had to race for their lives from the chasing shark!

Meanwhile, far away in Sydney, the diver had put Nemo in a fish tank in his dental office. The other fish were thrilled to meet him and made him part of the Tank Gang, nicknaming him, "Shark Bait." Gill was their leader. He had a plan for all the tank fish to escape, but they needed Nemo's help. And Nemo needed their help, too. The dentist was planning on giving Nemo to his niece, Darla. Darla had shaken her last fish to death! But the Tank Gang's plan to break the tank's filter failed and poor Nemo's life had been put in danger.

Back in the ocean, Marlin fought off a hideous anglerfish in the black depths of the ocean while Dory read the writing on the mask. It said: "P. Sherman, 42 Wallaby Way, Sydney." Some moonfish told them to follow the East Australian Current to get there.

On the way, Marlin and Dory were surrounded by hundreds of jellyfish – and Dory got stung. Marlin heroically pulled her to safety but not without getting stung himself. When he woke up, he discovered they had been rescued by a group of surfing turtles. The turtles listened to Marlin's amazing story and sent the message from turtle to fish to dolphin to seabird to... a pelican named Nigel in Sydney Harbour who was friends with the Tank Gang and knew Nemo!

Nigel flew to Dr Sherman's office and told Nemo the good news. Filled with pride that his dad was on the way to rescue him, Nemo gathered up his courage and managed to break the fish tank's filter with a pebble! Now the plan to escape was back in motion!

Dory and Marlin caught a ride in a whale's mouth all the way into Sydney Harbour, but when they got there, a pelican snapped them up in its bill for breakfast. Luckily, Nigel the pelican came to their rescue just in time and flew them to the dentist's window. Marlin saw Nemo in a plastic bag full of water, belly-up. Poor Marlin didn't realize Nemo was only pretending as part of his escape plan. Then the dentist shoved Nigel out the window. Marlin was heartbroken. Back in the harbor, he said goodbye to Dory and sadly began the long journey home alone.

Nemo's escape was not going according to plan. His bag sprung a leak and the dentist's niece had shaken him out onto the dental tray. The Tank Gang came to the rescue. Gill managed to shoot out of the tank and catapult Nemo down the spit sink – to freedom.

After making his way through the rapids at the water treatment plant, Nemo splashed into the ocean and met up with Dory. When she finally realized who he was, Dory helped Nemo find Marlin, who had swam into the fishing grounds. Marlin was delighted to see his son! But the celebration was short as Dory got caught in a giant fishing net! Convincing his father that he knew what to do, Nemo bravely swam inside the net and encouraged all the fish to swim down and break the net.
The plan worked!

Marlin was overjoyed to be with his son again. A few weeks later, safely back at home, Marlin and Nemo rushed to the schoolyard. Marlin knew at last that his son could look after himself. Before Nemo swam off with his class, he came back to give Marlin a big hug. "Love ya, Dad," said Nemo. "I love you, too, son," said Marlin.

The End